# sweet euphemism

# sweet euphemism

before/during/after internment
and all the generations between

ALISON LUBAR

**Grateful acknowledgments to the following:**
"They Won't Come Out" *White Wall Review,* 2022.
"Strawberry Harvest" first appeared as part of "(Re)Generation Triptych (1940-2019)," *Processing Crisis,* an anthology published by St. Mary's College of California, 2022.
"Just Desserts" was first published in *queer feast: making the bitter sweet,* with Bottlecap Press, 2022.
"Solidarity" was first published as "Hakone, 2009" with Five South in *The Weekly,* 2022.
"Practical Magic" was first published by *Foglifter,* 2023.

sweet euphemism



Mouthfeel Press is an indie press publishing works in English and Spanish by new and established poets. We publish poetry, fiction, and non-fiction. Our print books are available through our independent bookstores, website, Bookshop.org, and other online and independent booksellers, or at author's readings. Ebooks are available through KOBO.

Cover Art by Octavio Quintanilla
Art Title: Frontextos, Abstract Borderland 65
Cover Design: Karen Dreher

Contact Information:

Mouthfeelbooks.com
Info.mouthfeelbooks@gmail.com

Print ISBN: 978-1-957840-08-6
Ebook ISBN: 978-1-957840-09-3

Published in the United States, 2023
First Printing in English
$12

# table of contents

"Life is too short not to order the bacon dessert."
—George Takei

*for Auntie E, who always reminds me of how to stay wild*

# sweet euphemism

# Auntie, Refusing Baptism

*Tule Lake Relocation Center, 1944*

"The straight and narrow
was no life for me.

Not wanting to disappoint
my mother, but only the pastor,
I refused baptism.

      How could I live
the straight and narrow
      when I preferred
the wide and winding?

The path trampled and fed
with tributaries and branching
off to another place.

I didn't want a road, or even a map.
And besides, we couldn't even leave
the camp."

# They Won't Come Out

*Oakland CA, 2013*

Auntie circumvents direct
questions. She turns the camps

into the mild weather today, or
a sale at the fabric shop. But

when we get an Irish coffee
or share a wine tasting, she'll let the crack of light

under the doorway of memory show four students
running from the library dropping as each passes

the guard tower. Remembers the twitches and pages
flutter away up and over the barbed wire. Or school
named by number. Or the time a neighbor accused
her of stealing a golden eagle statuette. Or beating

the bully with an umbrella for the first time to prevent
a second. Or Jack, "who suffered the most" under
his father, as the oldest, emasculated, imprisoned. We sip
something fruity from Sonoma until the last dregs

dribble onto the woven cotton placemats. The next day
these dark red spots remain; they won't come out. She didn't escape

unscathed. Jack turned into a bear with blunted horse-teeth. She, into
a totem of birds, or a dragonfly mantle hovering above the lemon tree.

# Strawberry Harvest

*Tacoma WA, May 1940*

While they were picking strawberries,
I was listening for screams.

Every fifteen minutes,
as often as I would try to wait to run
to the bathroom to wash the sticky witness
of poverty from my hands,
the manual labor of a ten-year-old,
        I would listen for the screams
of women in the field
who came across
a garter snake.
        Helpless, the snake,
and helpless, the women,
and helpless, us who waited
        for a December
        to change our lives,

but for now, I pinch the strong,
thin stem and place
each freckled reminder of my life
in a basket.
        I save the good ones for the top,
        and the bruised sweat underneath,
        blemished by no fault of their own.

I am not unhappy. I wait for the screams,
better at picking snakes than strawberries.

# Auntie E, Cross–Country

*U.S. Highway 66, 1961*

Pocketbooks full
of scribbled digits
on bar napkins, we flee
each dive with a wink
and a wave (we'll never
give *them* a call). Our green
Beetle revs and peels—
we *told them* it had wings!

I roll down one glass eye
while Leona coaxes flight—
we merge and she takes it up
twenty more as the gasoline trail
of station wagons & eighteen-
wheelers sweeten the air.

"Eat our dust!"
we whip past a last
pickup-truck—
in the rearview it
shrinks to a blip
on Route 66.

Tonight, there are three
new notes turned to
a flurry of twenty-ish—
the age we seem (joy
ingests crows' feet
like a delicacy).

We dance
everywhere we go:
freedom's foliage
is a flutter
of numbers.

# Just Desserts

*Tennessee, 1970*

In the Smoky Mountains, I am sober.
The skid stops, tires grind on gravel,
the path whorled and looped like
a fingerprint. I almost go over. The edge
is right there. Climb to the empty passenger's side
and slide down. A little black sedan pulls over,
someone in billowing paisley opens the door.
I spill like a tipped laundry basket, a pile of denim
and silk. I pull the red bandana over my eyes—
it matches the VW Bug, matches what might have filled
the inside if we went over. I can see how my car
and I could just splat. "There must be a reason,"
my impromptu EMT trills. "I'm going
to eat dessert for breakfast every day
from now on." We laugh and survey
the external damage—none to see
and inside of me there's a seed of
possibility now that I will replant
in everyone I meet.

# One More and You're Out

*Oakland CA, 2014*

Two strikes is good for a pitcher and bad for a dog—
the orange warning in the bay window watches
the sheepdog-nemesis pass at six every day.

The inside sill is shredded with the desperate scratches
of Pepper, rescued Aussie mix and resident antagonist.
Auntie sews canvas blackout panels with lemons and eagles,
signs of growth and skyward escape, to shield Pepper
from this daily agitation, and certain war.

Irises sprout from the bench in front, next to
the perennial rosemary we never pick—the sheepdog
marks it for his own. Pepper reclaims it—a land war.

One day, Auntie is early and the sheepdog is late—
with a primal lunge, Pepper breaks the leash, a wrist, the skin
of the enemy and that's how strike two happened. (The first
was a shih tzu, whose response to treatment and insistence
on living spared Pepper, too.) The rescue dog and the old maid.

When no one else can bear to live with you, two negatives
cancel each other in perfect math. Pepper's last strike
was merely age. Auntie waits for her turn at bat.

# Generational Demons as Indigestion

*Suburban NJ, 2022*

"The rice was bad"
is a euphemism—
she has no bitterness.

Two glasses of prosecco
in a row turns to pins jumbling
in a tarnished peppermint tin.

I'll do anything not to throw up.
Bad stomachs are hereditary.
Auntie outlived the cancer. I get

little patches of scales. I am too nervous
to heal. There, they poisoned the rice. Here,
they don't need to bother. Any grandmother knows

flat ginger ale will neutralize norovirus. Saltine crackers
are the holy body that keeps intestinal peace. Really,
I don't feel that bad.

# Haibun for Running Into Your Ex

*San Francisco, 1957*

After the war, Granny and Auntie took care of the estate of Mr. Martin. Mrs. Martin's oil painting of her poodle still hangs across from Auntie's spot at the dining table. A bite-size Matisse wannabe with putrid ochre and violent yellow behind tufts of thick white curled fur, the frame is gold and wide. Mr. Martin was kind to Auntie, who confessed to pretending to be stupid so she could be mean. Made the Japanese-demon-face behind his back. Cut her nails onto his bedsheets. Left an errant hair under his napkin, as a curse. Granny was happy to have work. Smallness and otherness as ægis. But when she sees her abandoned husband in the Mission District,

He crosses the street,
looks down at the sidewalk cracks.
Ghosts never have teeth.

# Après–Camp, or, Retail Therapy

*San Francisco CA, 1948*

New socks with yellow-threadloop scalloped edges,
a spiral-bound notebook with hard cardboard cover,
then later a pack of marbled composition ones [their spots
like an ærial view of a crowded ranch and its jersey cows,
or somewhere dense, cramped and caged], a pœtry collection
or any number of paperback editions small enough to stow
in a pocketbook. Seed-beaded barrettes and a [black silk]
camisole. My mother [one day, Granny] sorts through
and chooses the nicest to ship back to Japan. "They have
nothing there." I start to only buy gifts [for myself]  too big
to ship. Fishermen's cabled sweaters, thick ecru knots like ships
[or gallows], encyclopedia volumes from the thrift store [I promise
myself to memorize J through K], combat boots [I choose
blue laces]. When she is gone, I revert to miniature, assemble
a dollhouse. Thimble trashcans. Bottlecap pie-tins. Cork vanity
stool, complete with cottonball tufted seat. A quilting square
for a flat sheet. I even wire its lights to flash, with a switch
[for signals]. Off, [on. Here,] gone.

# Very Cruel Race

*Oakland CA, 2001*

"Very cruel race," declares
an early 2000s romcom. The bumbling starlet
listens to her dashing crush, twirls
sun-colored hair. All her cuticles are chewed.
                  West-Coast twilight turns the two walls of windows
                        deep-ocean dark. Three generations of us sit
                  underneath the newly-installed flatscreen. My mother
            brings the DVD in her luggage, to give to Auntie afterward.
*Very cruel race* registers
                              like an underwater sonic boom. I laugh
                              on reflex. All of us nod and understand.
Once, Auntie beat another schoolkid
            with a yellow umbrella to prevent further bullying. Cruelty
                  is preventative, and it's better to let people know
                  where they stand. No furtive poisoning of rice,
                        no euphemistic relocation. This is before
                        I come out. This self-hate, internalized,
                  eats away like the stomach cancer Granny
            and her estranged husband died from. A coyote
      that chews off a leg to escape isn't cruel. The captive
      mouse that eats her pups. Fishing with a baseball bat.
Ending a marriage over the phone line of the rehab center.
At the end, the fair heroine gets her guy. Happily ever ever.

# Solidarity

*Hakone, 2009*

I had had enough herding
of Auntie through Tokyo
subway. We finally arrive
at the spa after a Pirate
Cruise. We order consomme
and something suspended
in aspic. Everything hovers
here: steam, gnats, sex-
lessness. I lock eyes with
someone with their own
older someone. We shrug
and spend the night taking
trips to the 711 down the hill
for onigiri and sake in little
egg-cups. We conjure Easter,
camaraderie, rebirth, and flirt.
The sun rises right on time
he leans in and I am all
rabbit-panic. Say my good-
bye and in our room, Auntie
is still up. "Now I know how
your father felt when you
were a teenager." I shower,
we never get to the spa, and
spend the whole bus ride
to Kyoto shrouded in a mix
of regret and affirmation. Some
things never change. I resume
my place to safeguard Auntie
as we usher from shrine to
shrine, avoid all indulgences
except for food. The rice is
the best here.

# Practical Magic

*Tule Lake Relocation Center, 1945*

We pass the golden eagle
statue back and forth, then hold
it between us. I am thirteen,
which must be lucky, since every-
thing they tell us is a lie. My mother
takes the cooking pot, drops
in one grain for every month
we've been here. Forty-one. With-
out rinsing, the water clouds
as starch and asbestos swirl.
We shred one page from
the dropped library book. No blood
from the student who was shot.
On each slip or square, we write
a name, or place. Like twenty
questions: animal (bear), vegetable
(strawberry), mineral (iron
barbed wire). We boil it to paste,
then paint the bottom jambs
with sticky translucence. It shines
pearlescent. "During every war,
they bring food to the onibaba
on the outskirts." Even the rude
children. Even the dogs. Even
all of the women (left behind).

# To sleep, perchance

*Oakland CA, 2019*

Auntie and Pepper snore baritone
on the faded loveseat, faces slack,

mouths-open, each a rotated question
mark, curled around a tasseled pillow

or Sudoku volume. Jet lag wants to
lull me supine, and I promise to fight

until at least nine. At least until
the sun gœs down. The after-dinner

nature documentary flashes sepia
and grey; pachyderm thunder

would rumble the coffee table
if the volume wasn't down so low.

Yellow subtitles broadcast: "The story
of elephants shouldn't be about ivory.

It should be about their teeth." Is all life
measured by death? How many heart-

beats I have left, or who here is
the closest to unbeing? The titans

stroll past a line of skulls, touch
a tender trunk to each one. I surrender

to my own temporary slumber, and on the way
to the guest bed, cover Auntie with the lap quilt

from my mother. Pepper gets a nose pat. I wonder
what dreams may come.

# An Ode on the E

*Oakland CA, 2025*

Auntie E keeps
the melody of the latter
letter. Aunt like on't, like
upon, not the picnic pest,
kitchen interloper, mistaken
for pepper in a dirty soup.
*I would eat it anyway,*
Auntie says, or shrugs and fishes
the drowning insect out,
administers microscopic
CPR. The E lives with infamy,
ineffable, eccentric. To be E,
*Most of my enemies and friends*
*are gone so I guess I've made*
*peace with the world.* The most
common vowel, impossible to escape.
She persists in euphemism, *The rice*
*was bad.* She has no bitterness
and still takes a slice of apple galette
for breakfast. I will give her a pre-
moniker, knighted title of "Ancient"
for her second hundred years.

# author's biography

Alison Lubar teaches high school English by day and yoga by night. They are a queer, nonbinary, mixed-race femme whose life work (aside from wordsmithing) has evolved into bringing mindfulness practices, and sometimes even poetry, to young people. Their work has been nominated for both the Pushcart & Best of the Net, and they're the author four chapbooks: *Philosophers Know Nothing About Love* (Thirty West Publishing House, 2022), *queer feast* (Bottlecap Press, 2022) and *it skips a generation* (Stanchion, Fall 2023). You can find out more at https://www.alisonlubar.com or on Twitter @theoriginalison.